He's fought Igyaks, fended off the Shrike-bats of Dromedon and remembers the day they inverted polarities, but how will the grizzled Autobot veteran Kup fare against this latest challenge—Zombots? Stranded on a desolate planet, alone and approaching shutdown fast, Kup fights off the hordes of evil and approaching insanity, but is everything as it seems...?

THE TRANSFORMERS: SPOTLIGHT
KUP

WRITTEN AND ILLUSTRATED BY: NICK ROCHE

COLORS BY: ANDREW ELDER

COVER ART BY: NICK ROCHE
& ALEX MILNE

LETTERS BY: ROBBIE ROBBINS

EDITS BY: CHRIS RYALL & DAN TAYLOR

Licensed by:

Hasbro

Properties Group

IDW

Special thanks to Hasbro's Aaron Archer, Elizabeth Griffin, Sheri Lucci, and Richard Zambarano for their invaluable assistance.

Spotlight

VISIT US AT
www.abdopublishing.com

Reinforced library bound edition published in 2008 by Spotlight, a division of the ABDO Publishing Group, 8000 West 78th Street, Edina, Minnesota 55439. Published by agreement with IDW Publishing. www.idwpublishing.com

Library of Congress Cataloging-in-Publication Data

Roche, Nick.
  Kup / written and illustrated by Nick Roche ; colors by Andrew Elder ; cover art by Nick Roche & Alan Milne ; letters by Robbie Robbins.
    p. cm. -- (The transformers: spotlight)
  ISBN 978-1-59961-475-5
  1. Graphic novels. I. Elder, Andrew. II. Title.
  PN6727.R59K87 2008
  741.5--dc22

                            2007033983

All Spotlight books have reinforced library bindings and are manufactured in the United States of America.

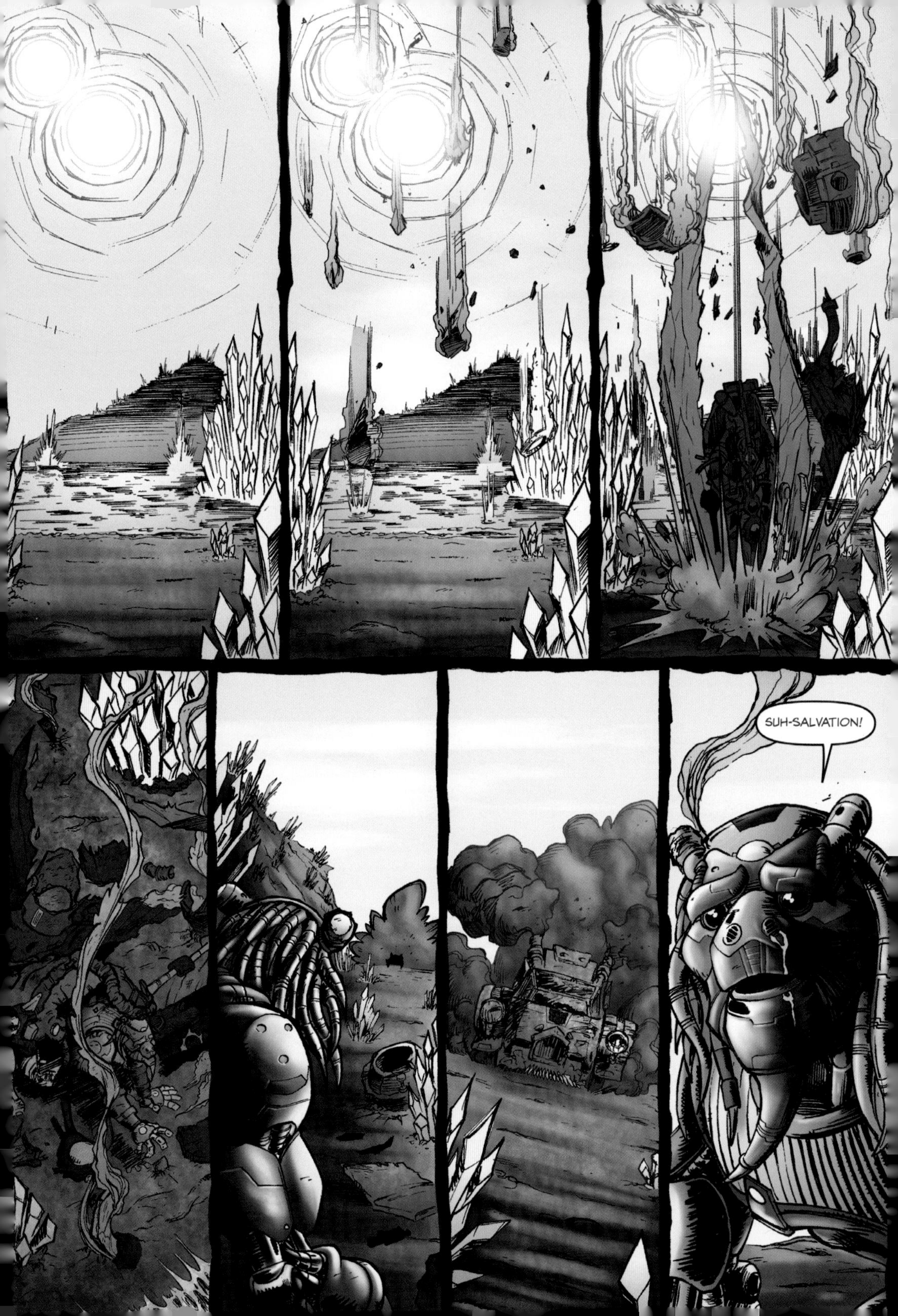
SUH-SALVATION!

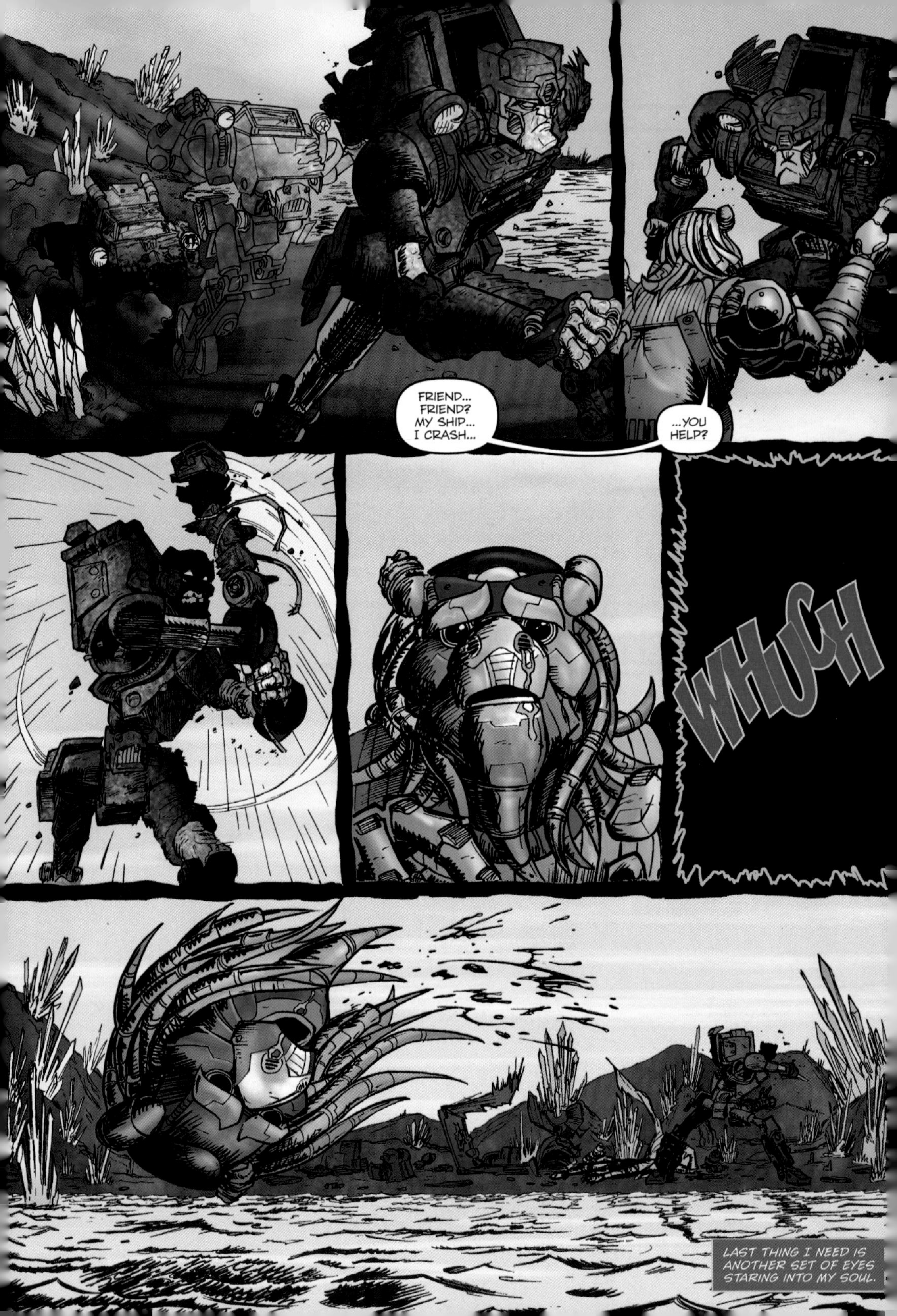
FRIEND... FRIEND? MY SHIP... I CRASH...
...YOU HELP?
WHUCH
LAST THING I NEED IS ANOTHER SET OF EYES STARING INTO MY SOUL.

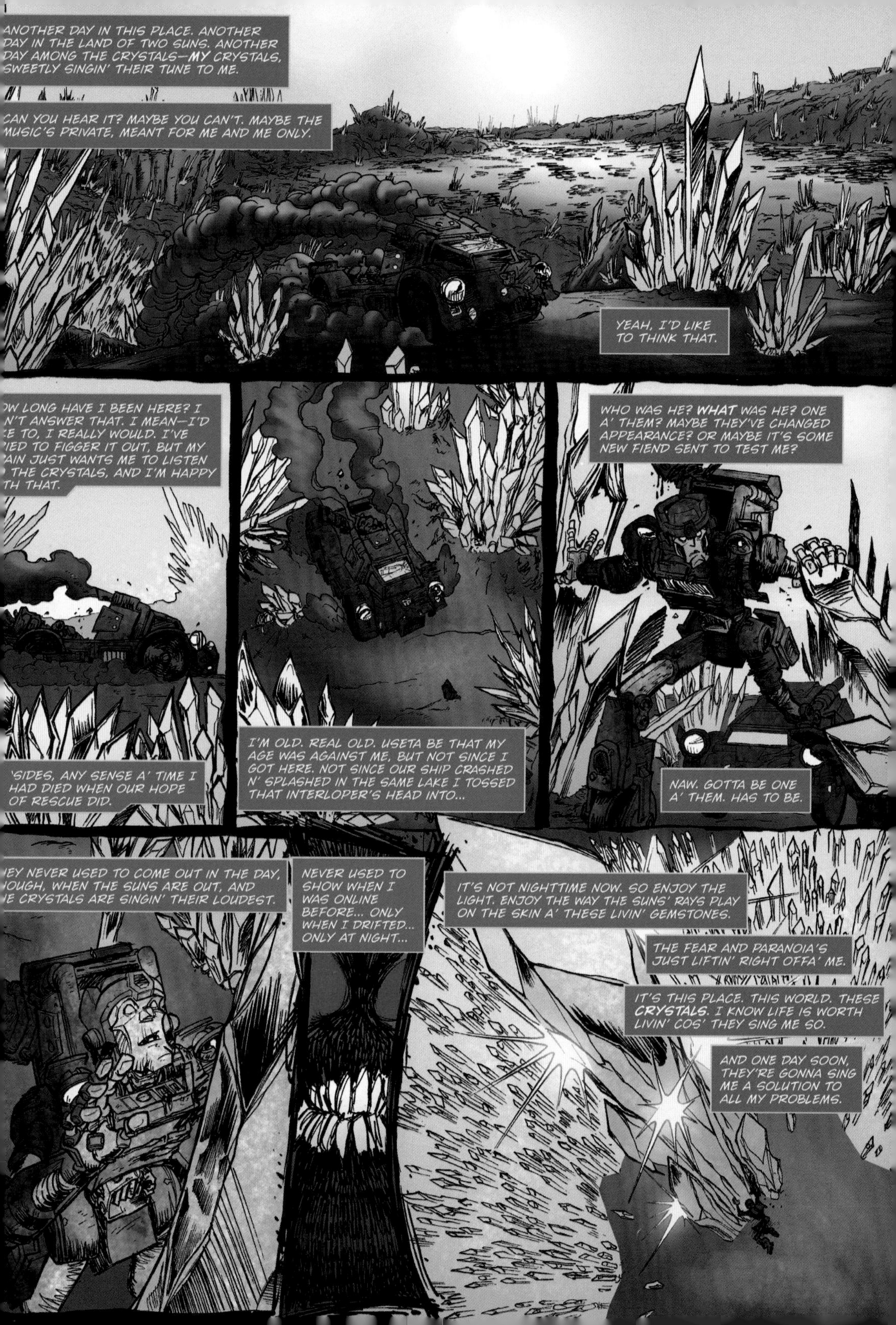
ANOTHER DAY IN THIS PLACE. ANOTHER DAY IN THE LAND OF TWO SUNS. ANOTHER DAY AMONG THE CRYSTALS—MY CRYSTALS, SWEETLY SINGIN' THEIR TUNE TO ME.
CAN YOU HEAR IT? MAYBE YOU CAN'T. MAYBE THE MUSIC'S PRIVATE, MEANT FOR ME AND ME ONLY.
YEAH, I'D LIKE TO THINK THAT.
OW LONG HAVE I BEEN HERE? I N'T ANSWER THAT. I MEAN—I'D E TO, I REALLY WOULD. I'VE IED TO FIGGER IT OUT, BUT MY AIN JUST WANTS ME TO LISTEN THE CRYSTALS, AND I'M HAPPY TH THAT.
'SIDES, ANY SENSE A' TIME I HAD DIED WHEN OUR HOPE OF RESCUE DID.
I'M OLD. REAL OLD. USETA BE THAT MY AGE WAS AGAINST ME, BUT NOT SINCE I GOT HERE. NOT SINCE OUR SHIP CRASHED N' SPLASHED IN THE SAME LAKE I TOSSED THAT INTERLOPER'S HEAD INTO...
WHO WAS HE? WHAT WAS HE? ONE A' THEM? MAYBE THEY'VE CHANGED APPEARANCE? OR MAYBE IT'S SOME NEW FIEND SENT TO TEST ME?
NAW. GOTTA BE ONE A' THEM. HAS TO BE.
EY NEVER USED TO COME OUT IN THE DAY, OUGH, WHEN THE SUNS ARE OUT, AND E CRYSTALS ARE SINGIN' THEIR LOUDEST.
NEVER USED TO SHOW WHEN I WAS ONLINE BEFORE... ONLY WHEN I DRIFTED... ONLY AT NIGHT...
IT'S NOT NIGHTTIME NOW. SO ENJOY THE LIGHT. ENJOY THE WAY THE SUNS' RAYS PLAY ON THE SKIN A' THESE LIVIN' GEMSTONES.
THE FEAR AND PARANOIA'S JUST LIFTIN' RIGHT OFFA' ME.
IT'S THIS PLACE. THIS WORLD. THESE CRYSTALS. I KNOW LIFE IS WORTH LIVIN' COS' THEY SING ME SO.
AND ONE DAY SOON, THEY'RE GONNA SING ME A SOLUTION TO ALL MY PROBLEMS.

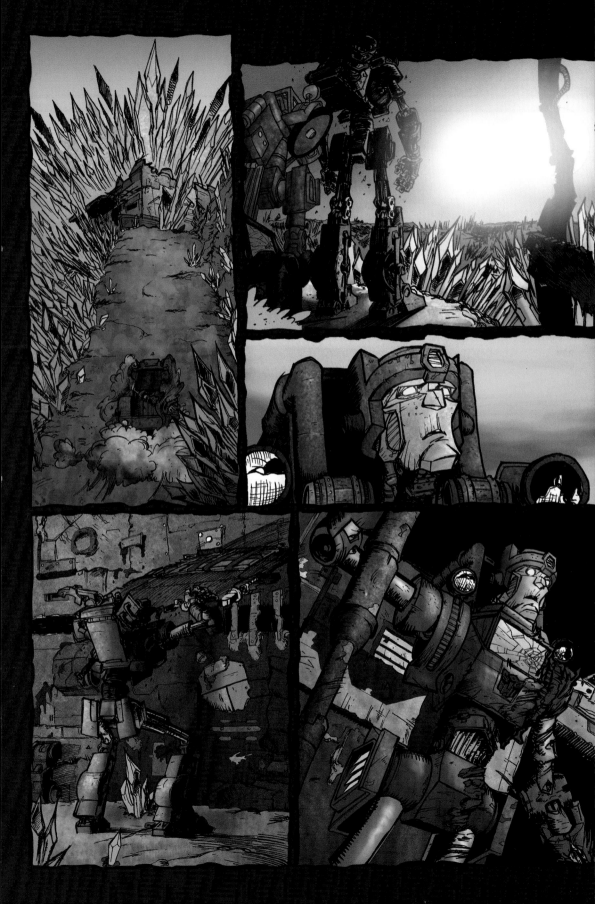

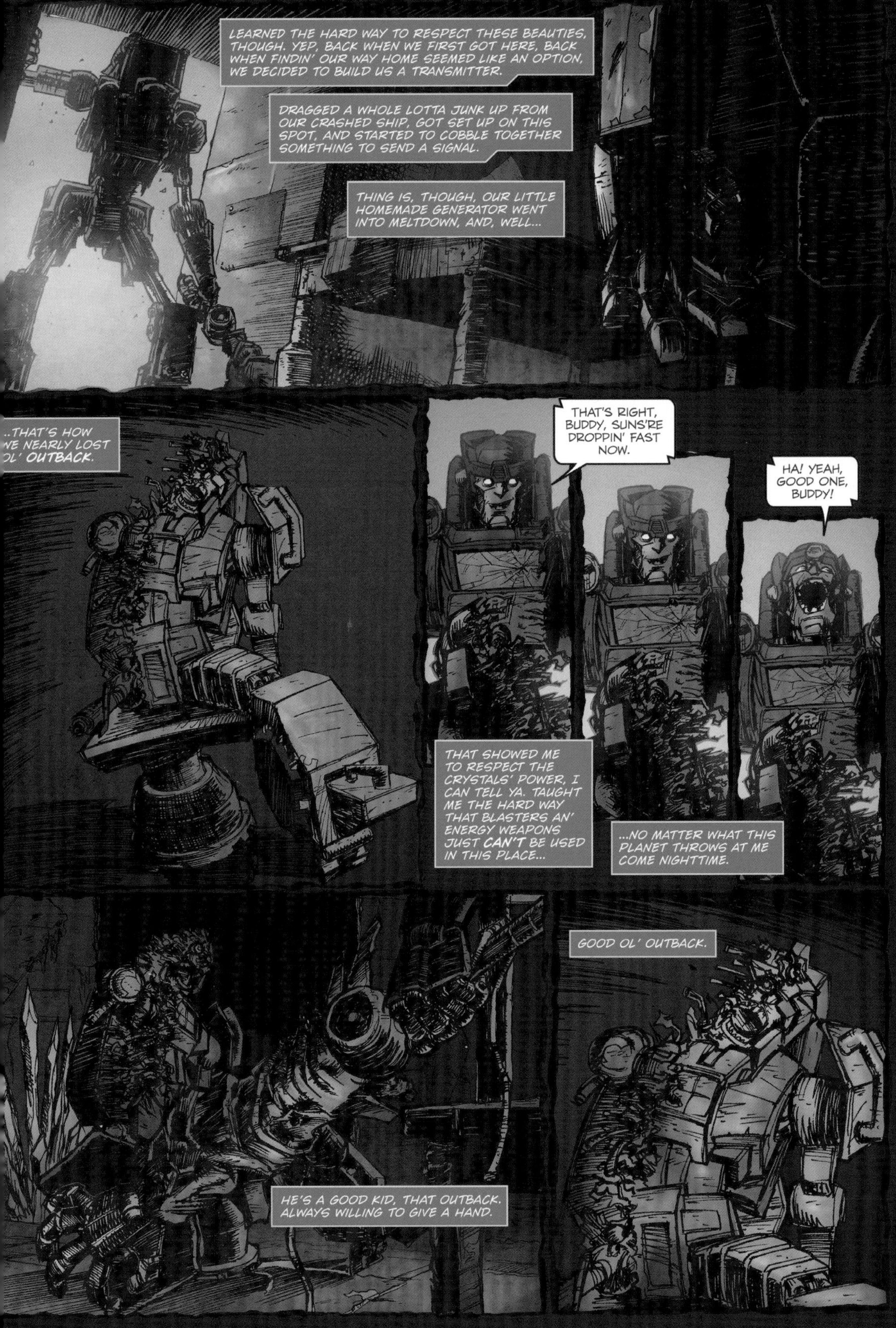
LEARNED THE HARD WAY TO RESPECT THESE BEAUTIES, THOUGH. YEP, BACK WHEN WE FIRST GOT HERE, BACK WHEN FINDIN' OUR WAY HOME SEEMED LIKE AN OPTION, WE DECIDED TO BUILD US A TRANSMITTER.
DRAGGED A WHOLE LOTTA JUNK UP FROM OUR CRASHED SHIP, GOT SET UP ON THIS SPOT, AND STARTED TO COBBLE TOGETHER SOMETHING TO SEND A SIGNAL.
THING IS, THOUGH, OUR LITTLE HOMEMADE GENERATOR WENT INTO MELTDOWN, AND, WELL...
..THAT'S HOW WE NEARLY LOST OL' OUTBACK.
THAT'S RIGHT, BUDDY, SUNS'RE DROPPIN' FAST NOW.
HA! YEAH, GOOD ONE, BUDDY!
THAT SHOWED ME TO RESPECT THE CRYSTALS' POWER, I CAN TELL YA. TAUGHT ME THE HARD WAY THAT BLASTERS AN' ENERGY WEAPONS JUST CAN'T BE USED IN THIS PLACE...
...NO MATTER WHAT THIS PLANET THROWS AT ME COME NIGHTTIME.
GOOD OL' OUTBACK.
HE'S A GOOD KID, THAT OUTBACK. ALWAYS WILLING TO GIVE A HAND.

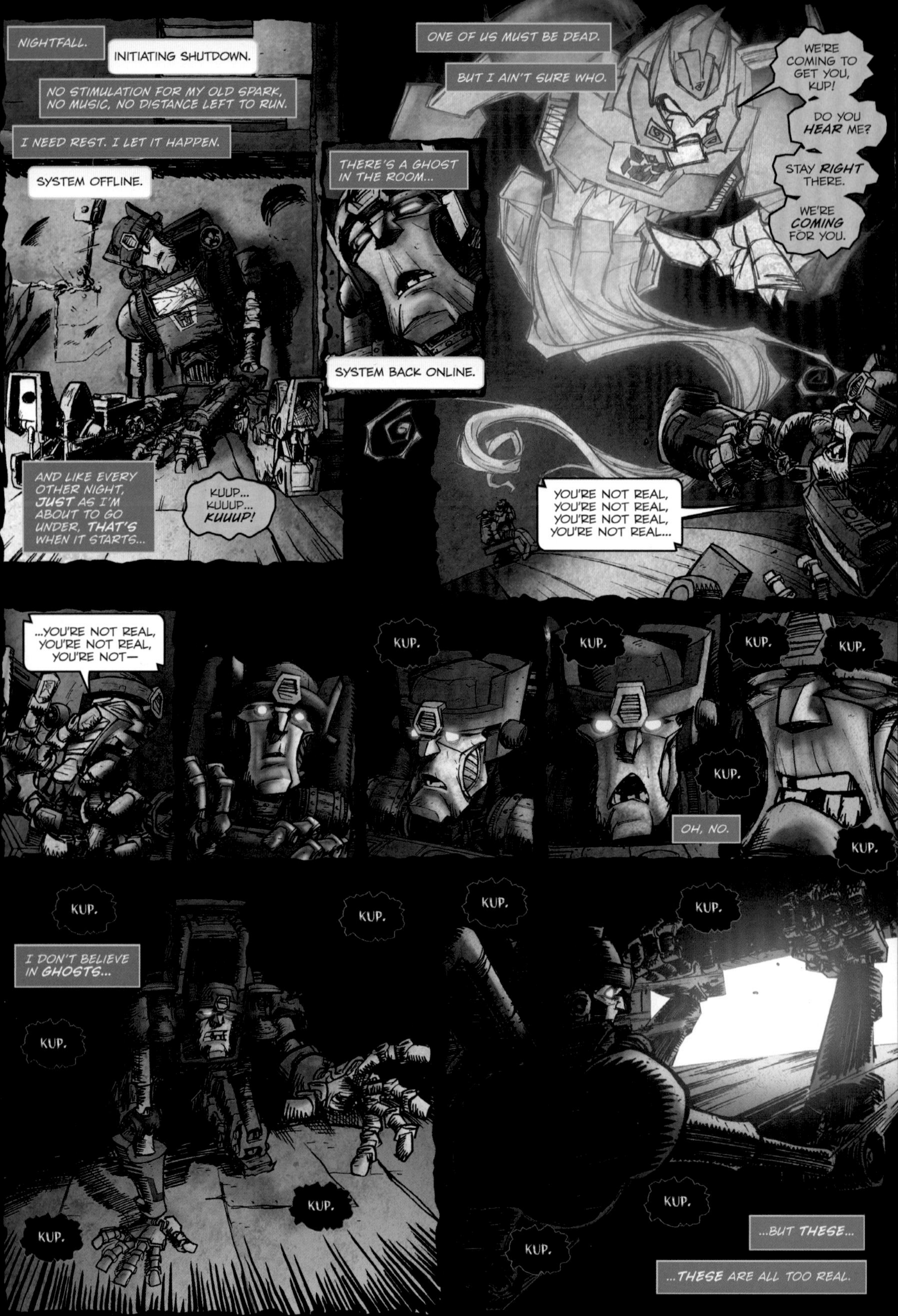

NIGHTFALL.
INITIATING SHUTDOWN.
NO STIMULATION FOR MY OLD SPARK, NO MUSIC, NO DISTANCE LEFT TO RUN.
I NEED REST. I LET IT HAPPEN.
SYSTEM OFFLINE.
AND LIKE EVERY OTHER NIGHT, JUST AS I'M ABOUT TO GO UNDER, THAT'S WHEN IT STARTS...
KUUP... KUUUP... KUUUP!
THERE'S A GHOST IN THE ROOM...
SYSTEM BACK ONLINE.
ONE OF US MUST BE DEAD.
BUT I AIN'T SURE WHO.
WE'RE COMING TO GET YOU, KUP!
DO YOU HEAR ME?
STAY RIGHT THERE.
WE'RE COMING FOR YOU.
YOU'RE NOT REAL, YOU'RE NOT REAL, YOU'RE NOT REAL, YOU'RE NOT REAL...
...YOU'RE NOT REAL, YOU'RE NOT REAL, YOU'RE NOT—
KUP.
KUP.
KUP.
KUP.
KUP.
OH, NO.
KUP.
KUP.
KUP.
KUP.
KUP.
I DON'T BELIEVE IN GHOSTS...
KUP.
KUP.
KUP.
KUP.
KUP.
...BUT THESE...
...THESE ARE ALL TOO REAL.

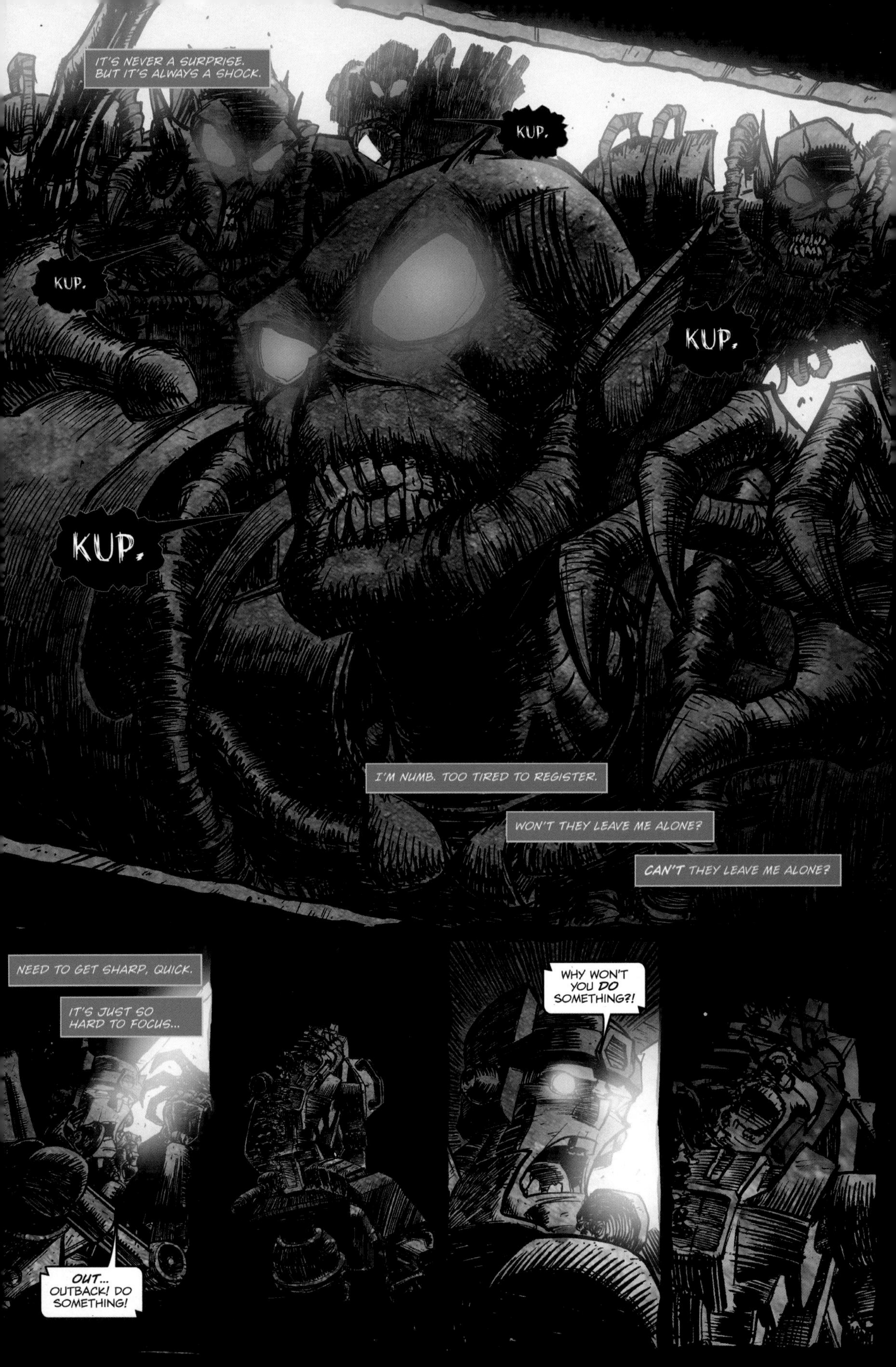

IT'S NEVER A SURPRISE. BUT IT'S ALWAYS A SHOCK.
KUP.
KUP.
KUP.
KUP.
I'M NUMB. TOO TIRED TO REGISTER.
WON'T THEY LEAVE ME ALONE?
CAN'T THEY LEAVE ME ALONE?
NEED TO GET SHARP, QUICK.
IT'S JUST SO HARD TO FOCUS...
OUT... OUTBACK! DO SOMETHING!
WHY WON'T YOU DO SOMETHING?!

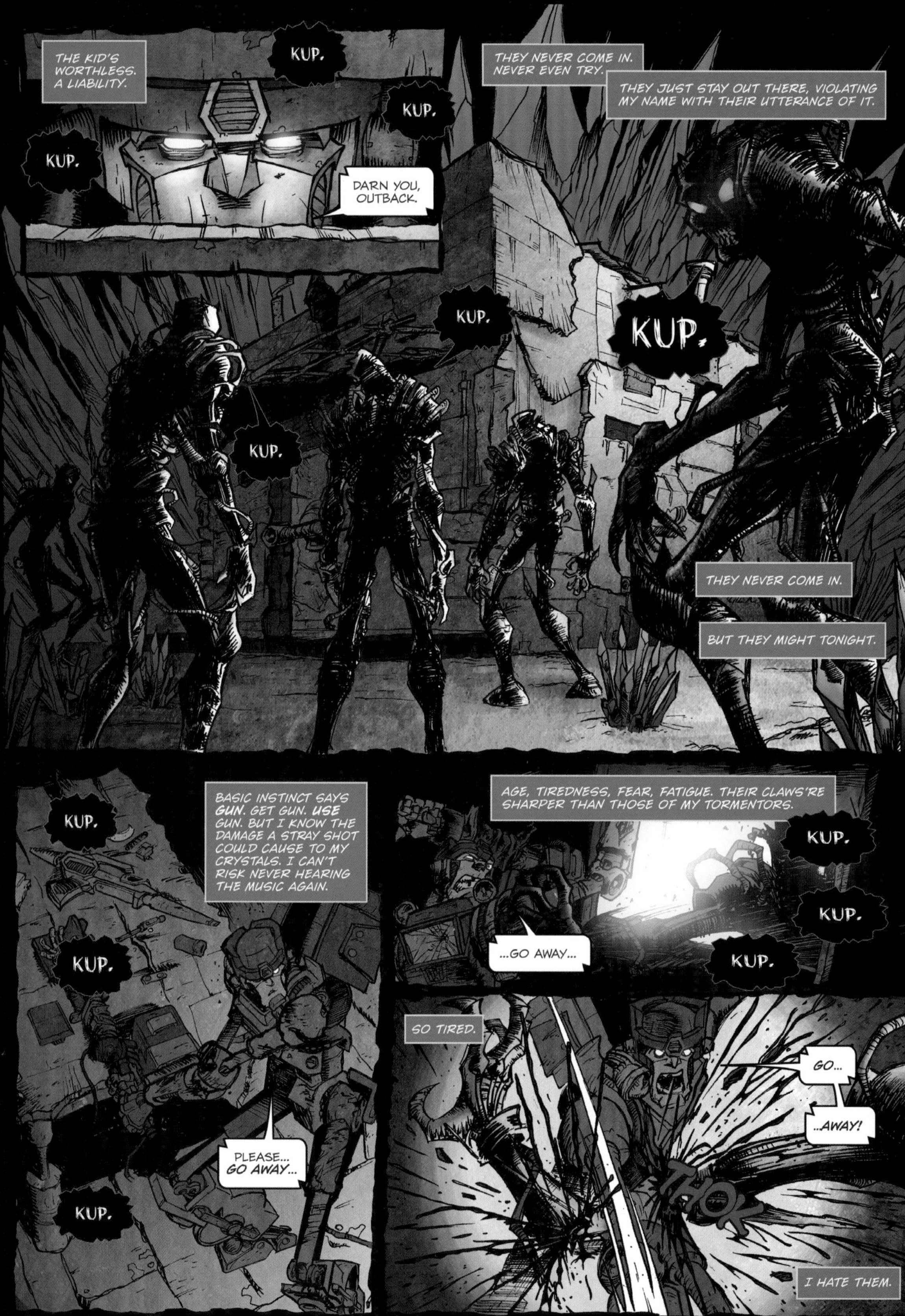
THE KID'S WORTHLESS. A LIABILITY.
KUP.
KUP.
KUP.
DARN YOU, OUTBACK.
THEY NEVER COME IN. NEVER EVEN TRY.
THEY JUST STAY OUT THERE, VIOLATING MY NAME WITH THEIR UTTERANCE OF IT.
KUP.
KUP.
KUP.
THEY NEVER COME IN.
BUT THEY MIGHT TONIGHT.
KUP.
BASIC INSTINCT SAYS GUN. GET GUN. USE GUN. BUT I KNOW THE DAMAGE A STRAY SHOT COULD CAUSE TO MY CRYSTALS. I CAN'T RISK NEVER HEARING THE MUSIC AGAIN.
KUP.
PLEASE... GO AWAY...
KUP.
AGE, TIREDNESS, FEAR, FATIGUE. THEIR CLAWS'RE SHARPER THAN THOSE OF MY TORMENTORS.
KUP.
KUP.
...GO AWAY...
KUP.
SO TIRED.
GO...
...AWAY!
THOK
I HATE THEM.

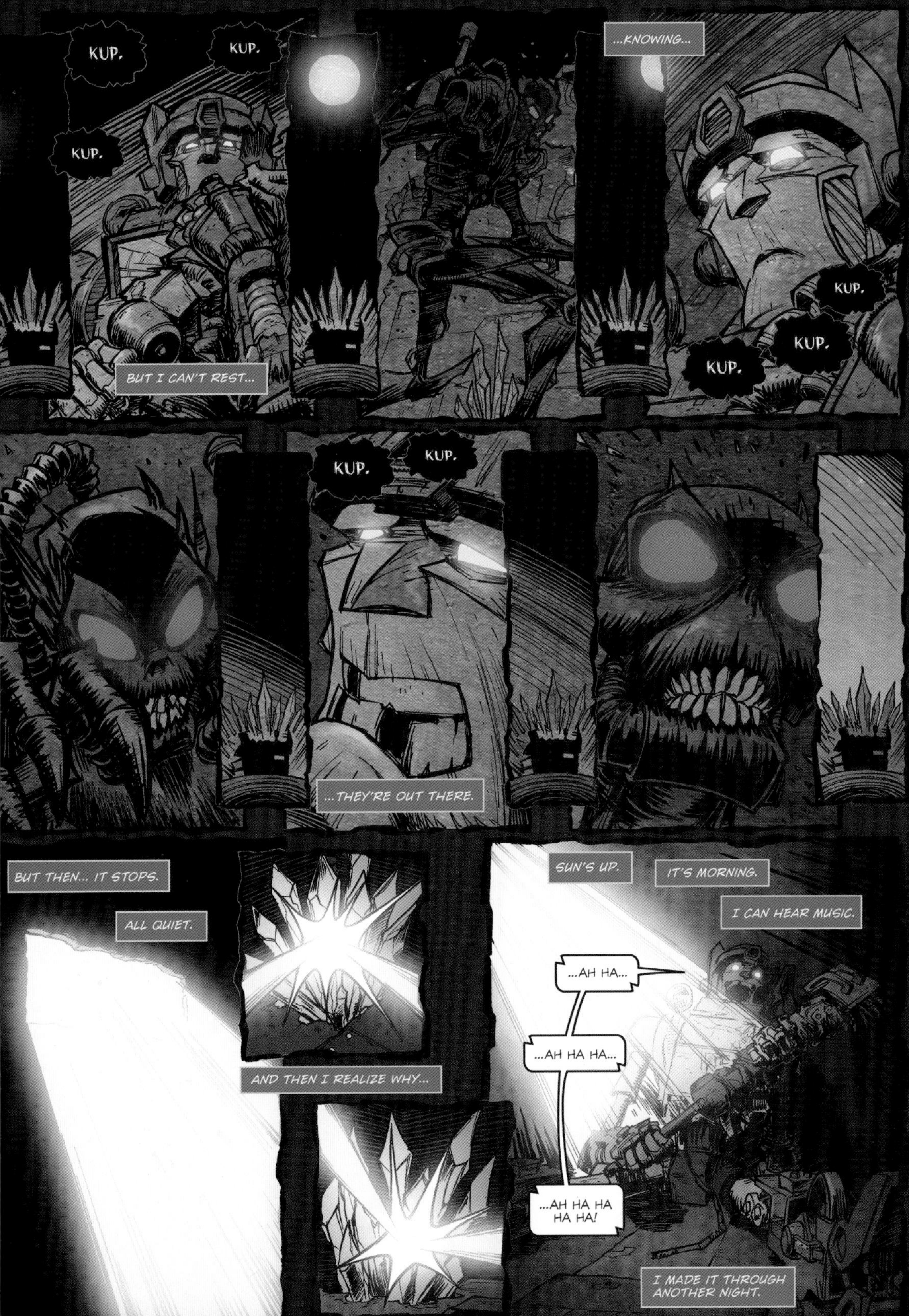
KUP.
KUP.
KUP.
BUT I CAN'T REST...
...KNOWING...
KUP.
KUP.
KUP.
KUP.
KUP.
...THEY'RE OUT THERE.
BUT THEN... IT STOPS.
ALL QUIET.
AND THEN I REALIZE WHY...
SUN'S UP.
IT'S MORNING.
I CAN HEAR MUSIC.
...AH HA...
...AH HA HA...
...AH HA HA HA HA!
I MADE IT THROUGH ANOTHER NIGHT.

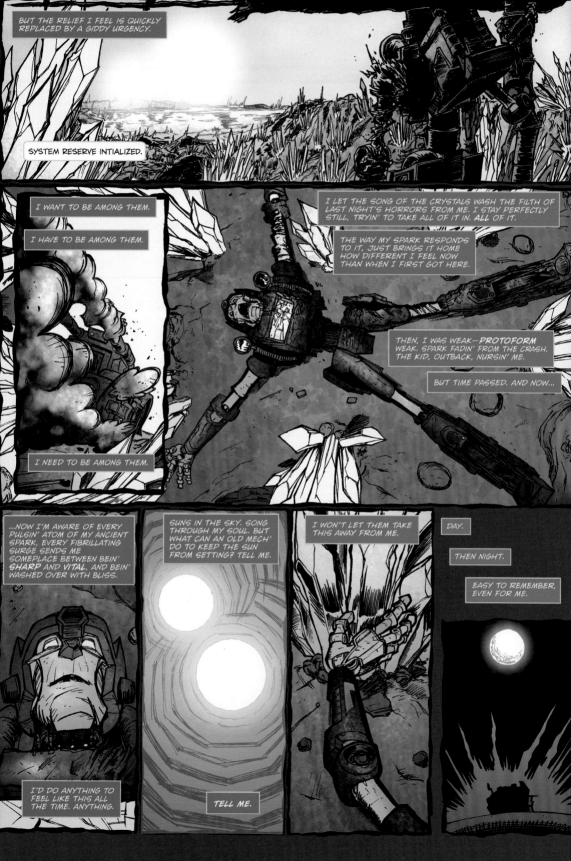

BUT THE RELIEF I FEEL IS QUICKLY REPLACED BY A GIDDY URGENCY.

SYSTEM RESERVE INTIALIZED.

I WANT TO BE AMONG THEM.

I HAVE TO BE AMONG THEM.

I NEED TO BE AMONG THEM.

I LET THE SONG OF THE CRYSTALS WASH THE FILTH OF LAST NIGHT'S HORRORS FROM ME. I STAY PERFECTLY STILL, TRYIN' TO TAKE ALL OF IT IN. *ALL* OF IT.

THE WAY MY SPARK RESPONDS TO IT, JUST BRINGS IT HOME HOW DIFFERENT I FEEL NOW THAN WHEN I FIRST GOT HERE.

THEN, I WAS WEAK—**PROTOFORM** WEAK. SPARK FADIN' FROM THE CRASH. THE KID, OUTBACK, NURSIN' ME.

BUT TIME PASSED. AND NOW...

...NOW I'M AWARE OF EVERY PULSIN' ATOM OF MY ANCIENT SPARK, EVERY FIBRILLATING SURGE SENDS ME SOMEPLACE BETWEEN BEIN' *SHARP* AND *VITAL*, AND BEIN' WASHED OVER WITH BLISS.

I'D DO ANYTHING TO FEEL LIKE THIS ALL THE TIME. ANYTHING.

SUNS IN THE SKY. SONG THROUGH MY SOUL. BUT WHAT CAN AN OLD MECH' DO TO KEEP THE SUN FROM SETTING? TELL ME.

TELL ME.

I WON'T LET THEM TAKE THIS AWAY FROM ME.

DAY.

THEN NIGHT.

EASY TO REMEMBER, EVEN FOR ME.

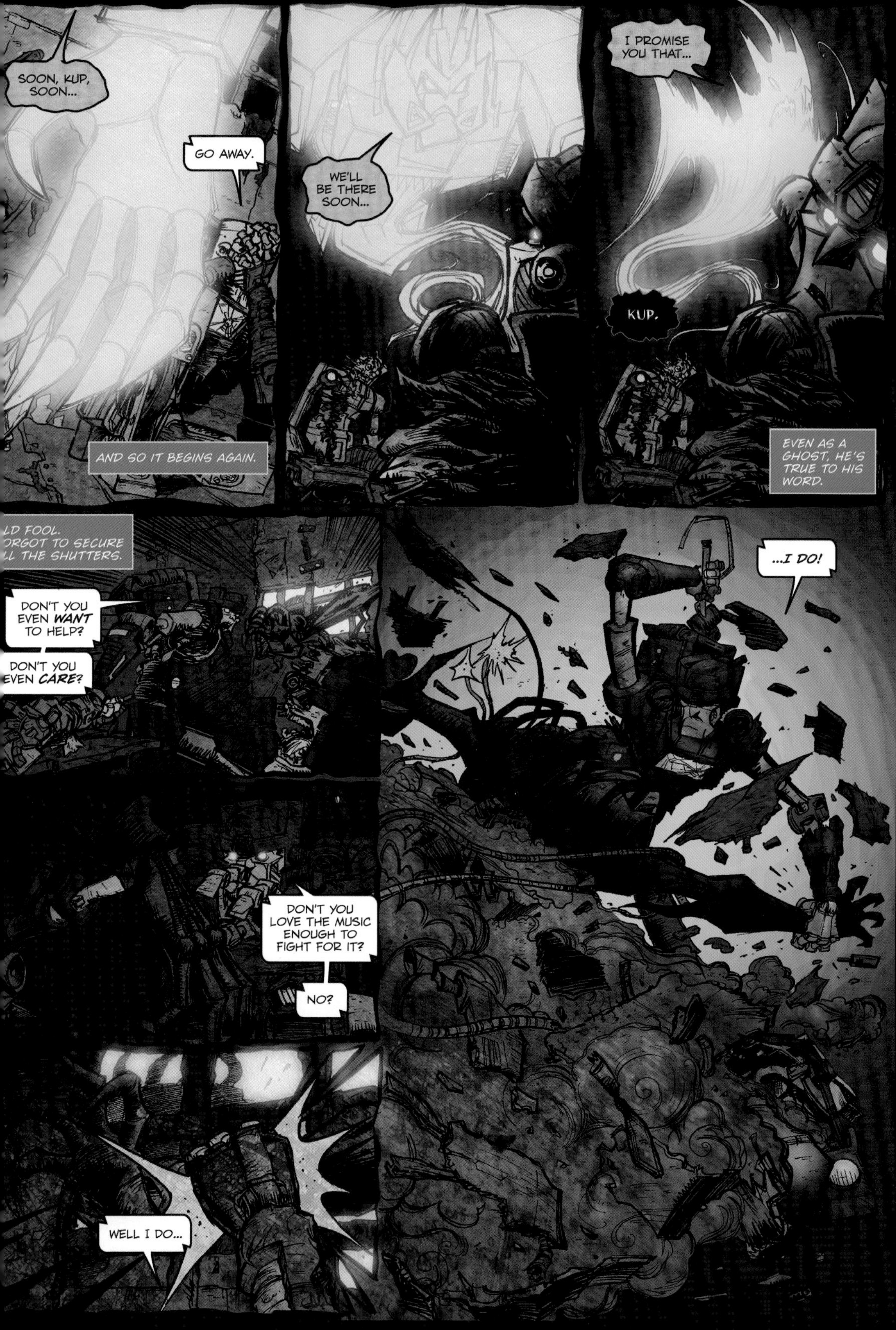
SOON, KUP, SOON...
GO AWAY.
AND SO IT BEGINS AGAIN.
WE'LL BE THERE SOON...
I PROMISE YOU THAT...
KUP.
EVEN AS A GHOST, HE'S TRUE TO HIS WORD.
LD FOOL. ORGOT TO SECURE LL THE SHUTTERS.
DON'T YOU EVEN WANT TO HELP?
DON'T YOU EVEN CARE?
DON'T YOU LOVE THE MUSIC ENOUGH TO FIGHT FOR IT?
NO?
WELL I DO...
...I DO!

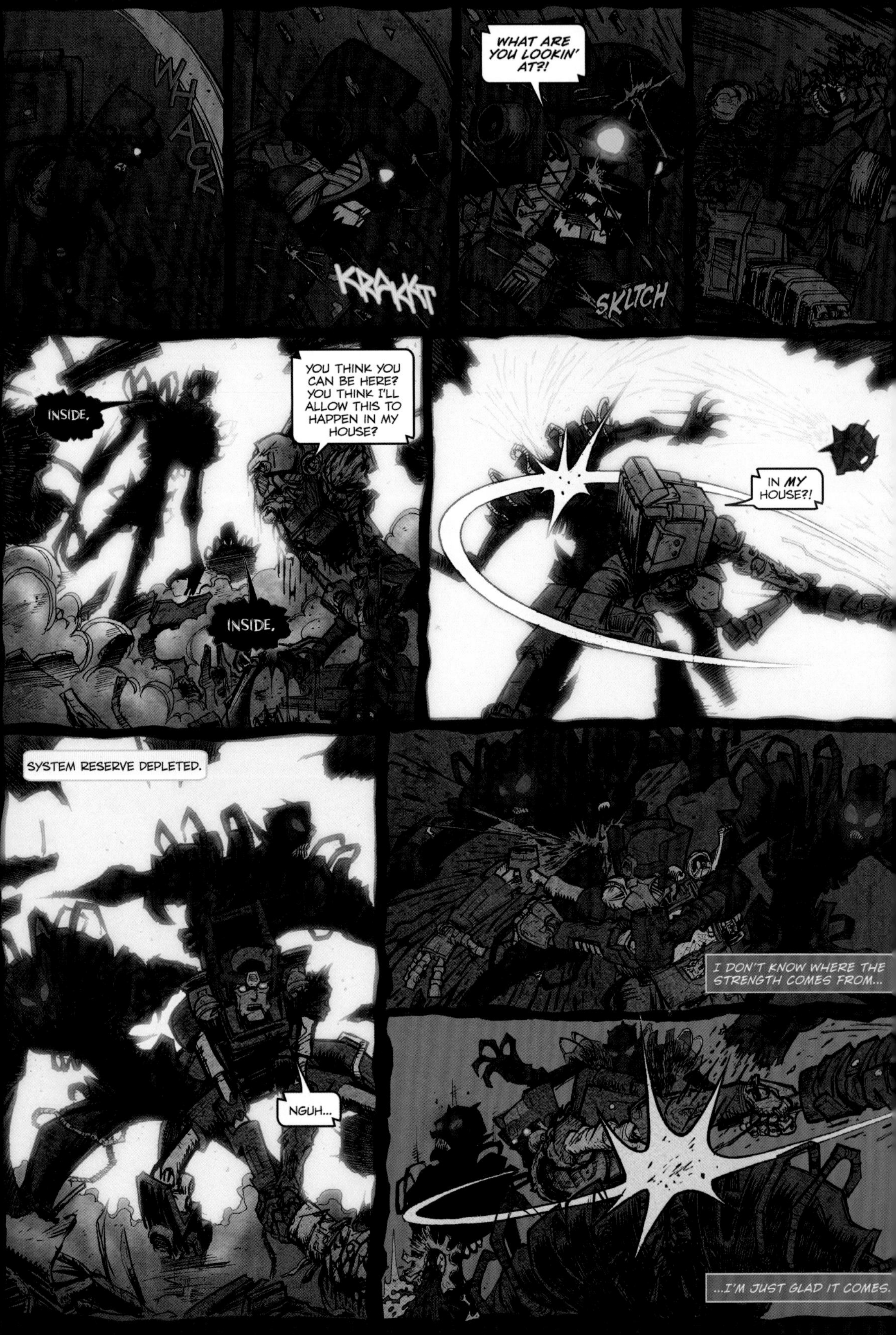
WHACK
KRAKKT
WHAT ARE YOU LOOKIN' AT?!
SKLTCH
INSIDE.
YOU THINK YOU CAN BE HERE? YOU THINK I'LL ALLOW THIS TO HAPPEN IN MY HOUSE?
INSIDE.
IN MY HOUSE?!
SYSTEM RESERVE DEPLETED.
NGUH...
I DON'T KNOW WHERE THE STRENGTH COMES FROM...
...I'M JUST GLAD IT COMES.

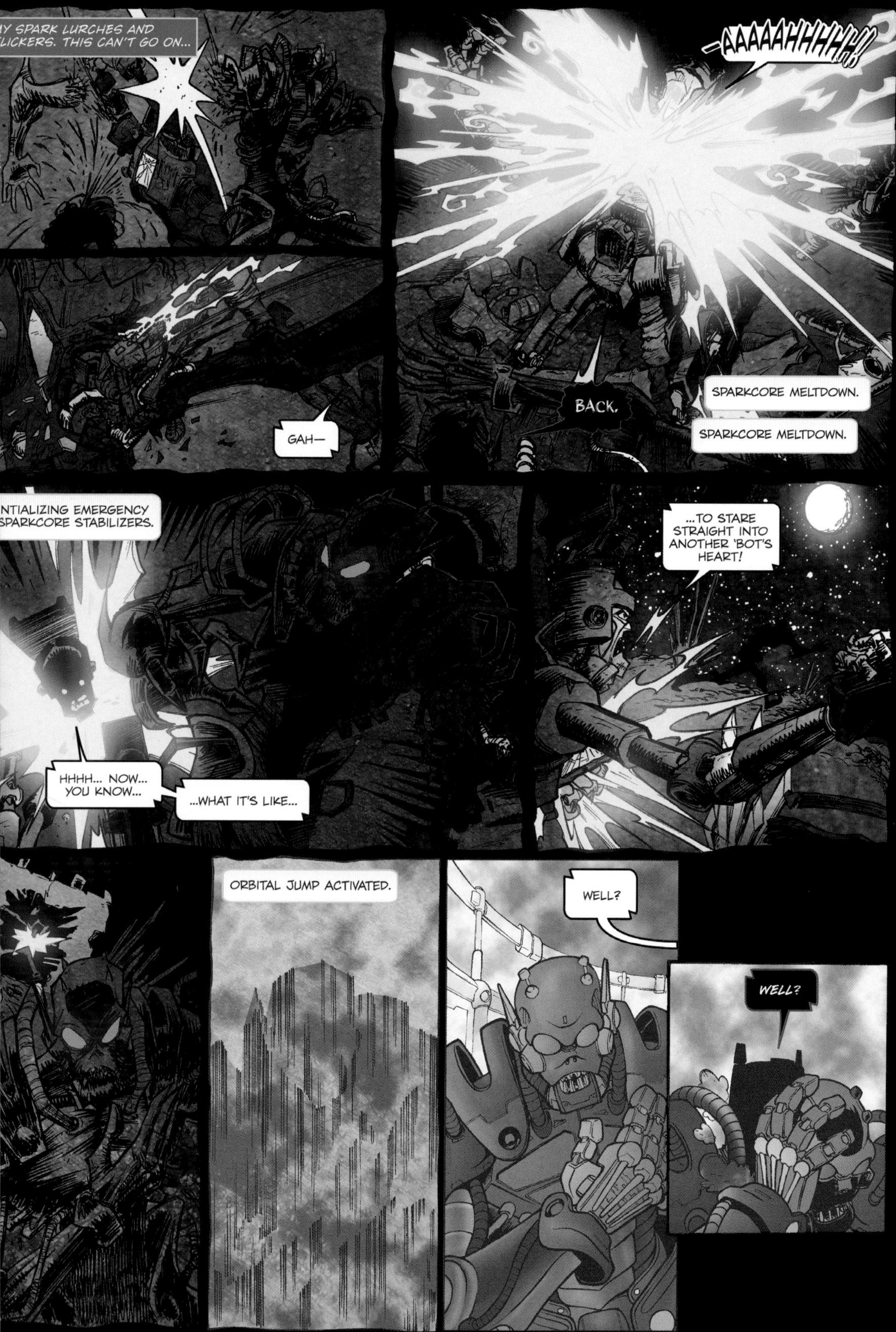
MY SPARK LURCHES AND FLICKERS. THIS CAN'T GO ON...
-AAAAAHHHH!!
GAH—
BACK.
SPARKCORE MELTDOWN.
SPARKCORE MELTDOWN.
INTIALIZING EMERGENCY SPARKCORE STABILIZERS.
HHHH... NOW... YOU KNOW...
...WHAT IT'S LIKE...
...TO STARE STRAIGHT INTO ANOTHER 'BOT'S HEART!
ORBITAL JUMP ACTIVATED.
WELL?
WELL?

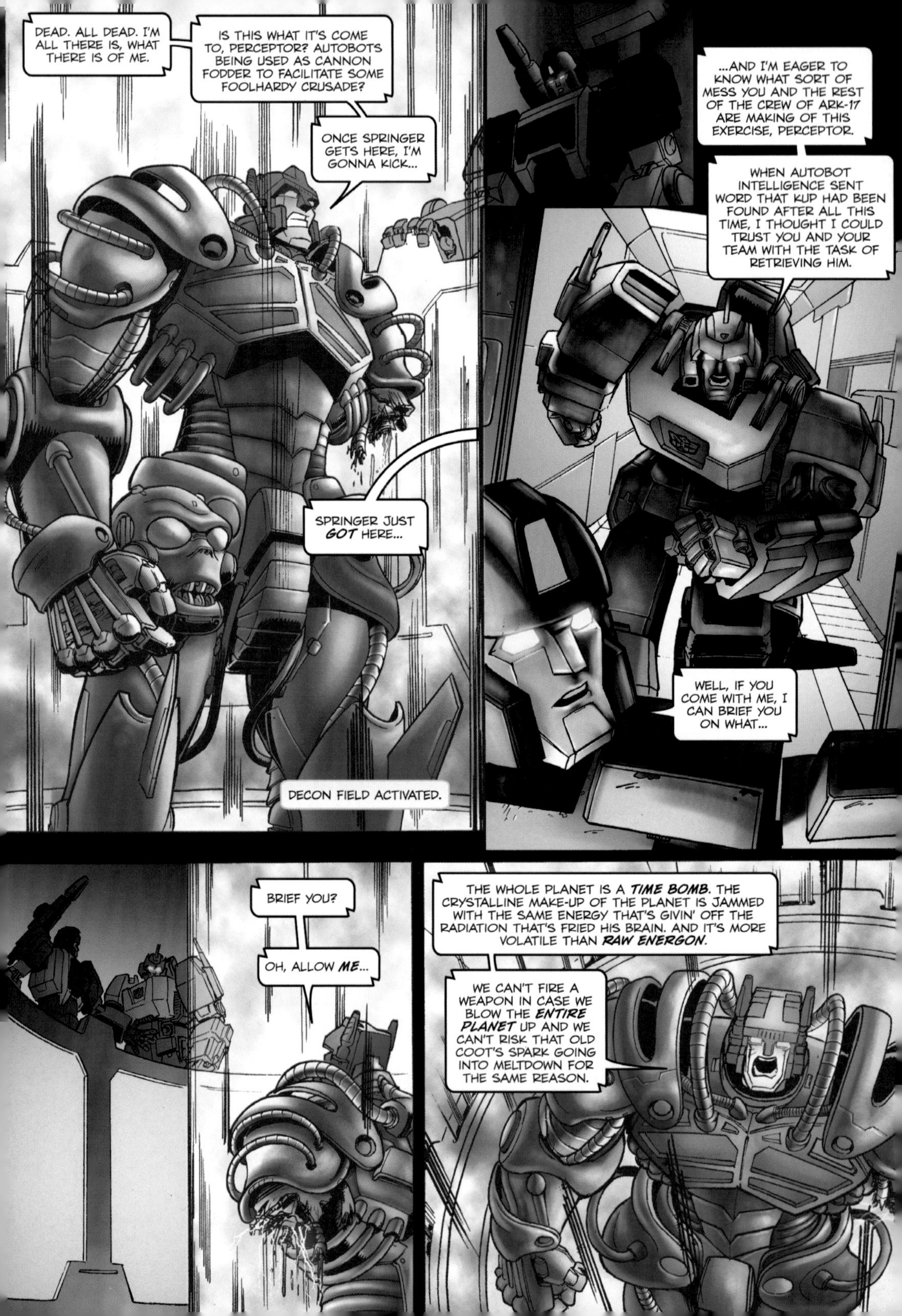
DEAD. ALL DEAD. I'M ALL THERE IS, WHAT THERE IS OF ME.
IS THIS WHAT IT'S COME TO, PERCEPTOR? AUTOBOTS BEING USED AS CANNON FODDER TO FACILITATE SOME FOOLHARDY CRUSADE?
ONCE SPRINGER GETS HERE, I'M GONNA KICK...
SPRINGER JUST *GOT* HERE...
DECON FIELD ACTIVATED.
...AND I'M EAGER TO KNOW WHAT SORT OF MESS YOU AND THE REST OF THE CREW OF ARK-17 ARE MAKING OF THIS EXERCISE, PERCEPTOR.
WHEN AUTOBOT INTELLIGENCE SENT WORD THAT KUP HAD BEEN FOUND AFTER ALL THIS TIME, I THOUGHT I COULD TRUST YOU AND YOUR TEAM WITH THE TASK OF RETRIEVING HIM.
WELL, IF YOU COME WITH ME, I CAN BRIEF YOU ON WHAT...
BRIEF YOU?
OH, ALLOW *ME*...
THE WHOLE PLANET IS A ***TIME BOMB***. THE CRYSTALLINE MAKE-UP OF THE PLANET IS JAMMED WITH THE SAME ENERGY THAT'S GIVIN' OFF THE RADIATION THAT'S FRIED HIS BRAIN. AND IT'S MORE VOLATILE THAN ***RAW ENERGON***.
WE CAN'T FIRE A WEAPON IN CASE WE BLOW THE ***ENTIRE PLANET*** UP AND WE CAN'T RISK THAT OLD COOT'S SPARK GOING INTO MELTDOWN FOR THE SAME REASON.

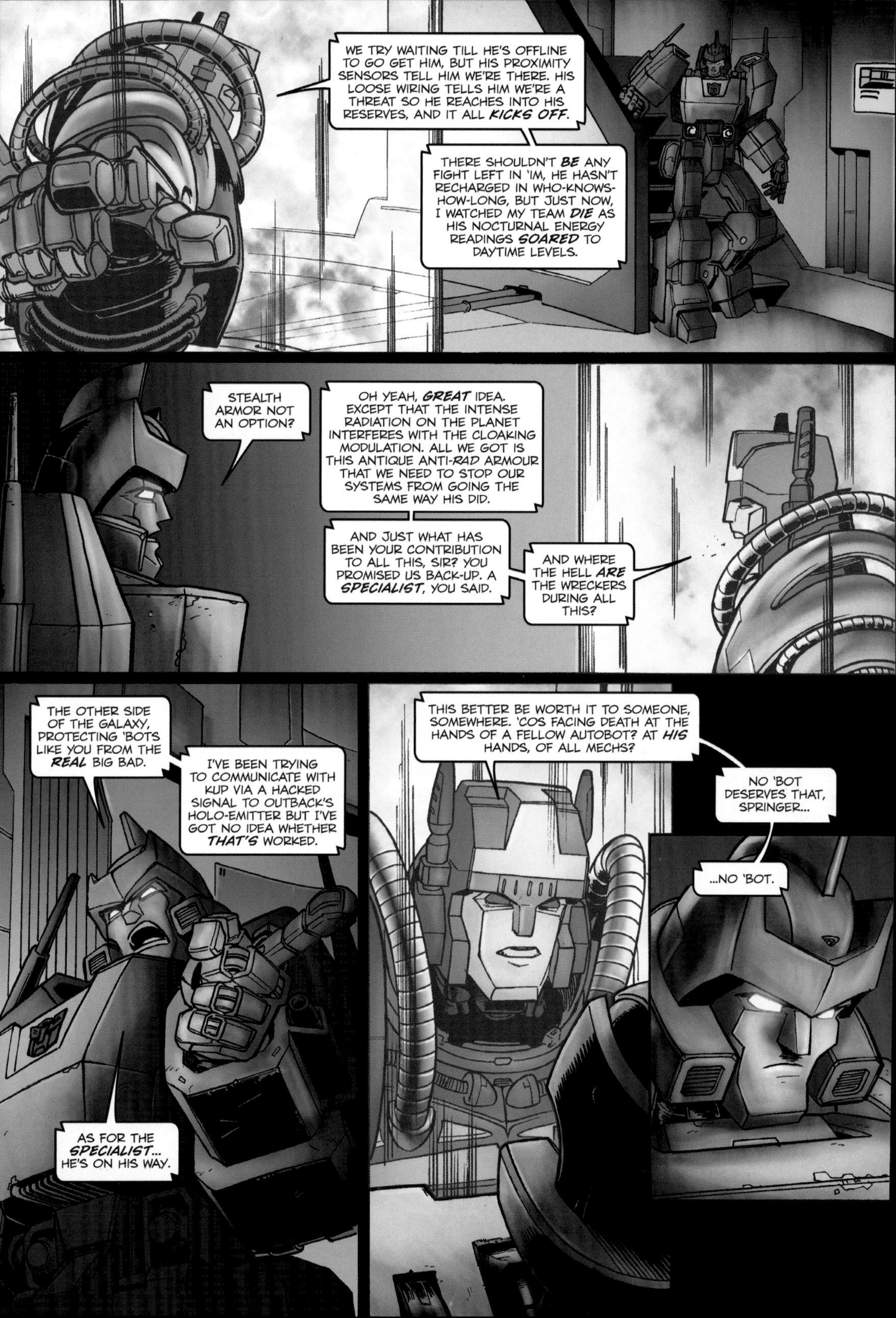
WE TRY WAITING TILL HE'S OFFLINE TO GO GET HIM, BUT HIS PROXIMITY SENSORS TELL HIM WE'RE THERE. HIS LOOSE WIRING TELLS HIM WE'RE A THREAT SO HE REACHES INTO HIS RESERVES, AND IT ALL *KICKS OFF*.
THERE SHOULDN'T *BE* ANY FIGHT LEFT IN 'IM, HE HASN'T RECHARGED IN WHO-KNOWS-HOW-LONG, BUT JUST NOW, I WATCHED MY TEAM *DIE* AS HIS NOCTURNAL ENERGY READINGS *SOARED* TO DAYTIME LEVELS.
STEALTH ARMOR NOT AN OPTION?
OH YEAH, *GREAT* IDEA. EXCEPT THAT THE INTENSE RADIATION ON THE PLANET INTERFERES WITH THE CLOAKING MODULATION. ALL WE GOT IS THIS ANTIQUE ANTI-*RAD* ARMOUR THAT WE NEED TO STOP OUR SYSTEMS FROM GOING THE SAME WAY HIS DID.
AND JUST WHAT HAS BEEN YOUR CONTRIBUTION TO ALL THIS, SIR? YOU PROMISED US BACK-UP. A *SPECIALIST*, YOU SAID.
AND WHERE THE HELL *ARE* THE WRECKERS DURING ALL THIS?
THE OTHER SIDE OF THE GALAXY, PROTECTING 'BOTS LIKE YOU FROM THE *REAL* BIG BAD.
I'VE BEEN TRYING TO COMMUNICATE WITH KUP VIA A HACKED SIGNAL TO OUTBACK'S HOLO-EMITTER BUT I'VE GOT NO IDEA WHETHER *THAT'S* WORKED.
AS FOR THE *SPECIALIST*... HE'S ON HIS WAY.
THIS BETTER BE WORTH IT TO SOMEONE, SOMEWHERE. 'COS FACING DEATH AT THE HANDS OF A FELLOW AUTOBOT? AT *HIS* HANDS, OF ALL MECHS?
NO 'BOT DESERVES THAT, SPRINGER...
...NO 'BOT.

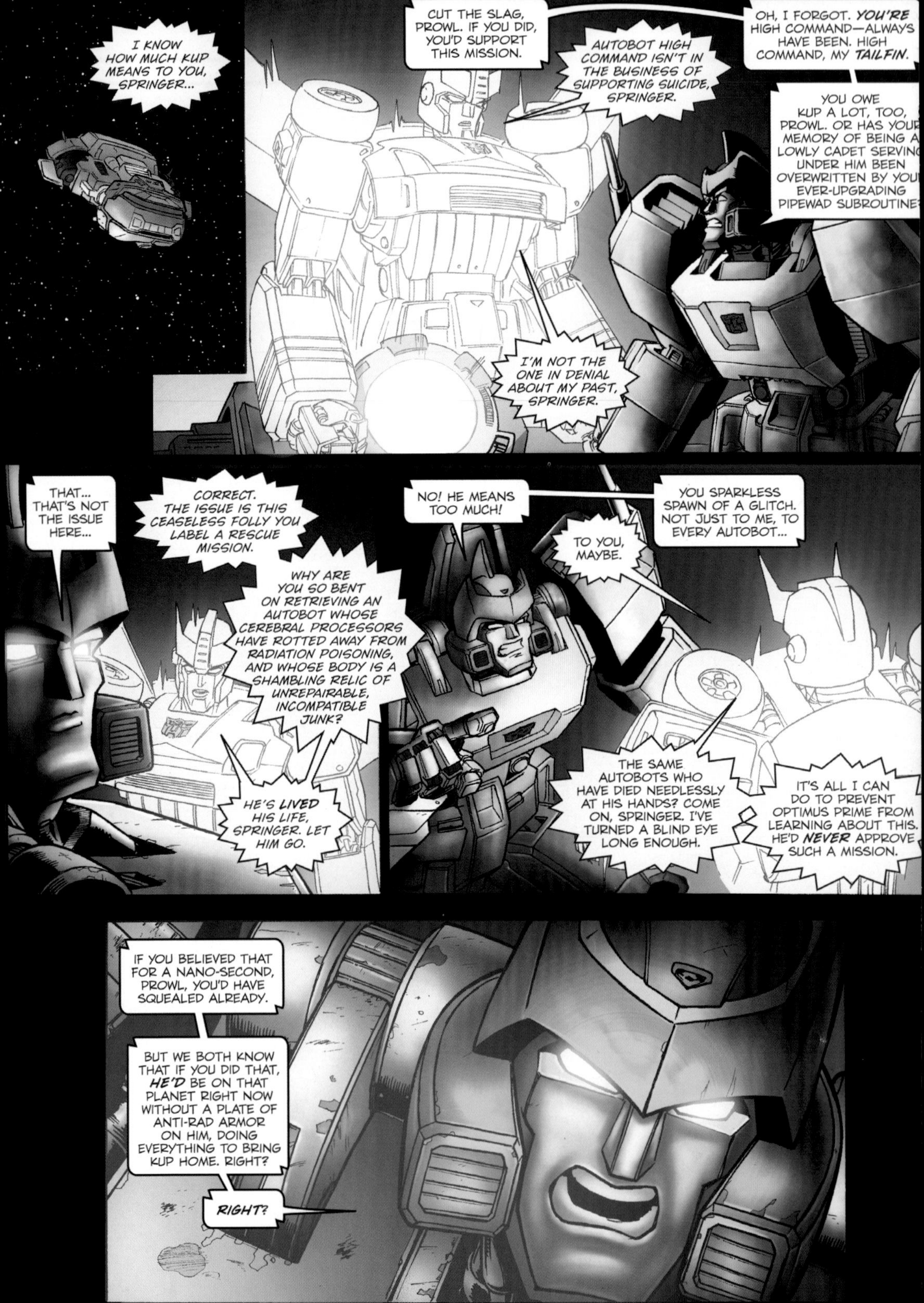
I KNOW HOW MUCH KUP MEANS TO YOU, SPRINGER...
CUT THE SLAG, PROWL. IF YOU DID, YOU'D SUPPORT THIS MISSION.
AUTOBOT HIGH COMMAND ISN'T IN THE BUSINESS OF SUPPORTING SUICIDE, SPRINGER.
OH, I FORGOT. ***YOU'RE*** HIGH COMMAND—ALWAYS HAVE BEEN. HIGH COMMAND, MY ***TAILFIN***.
YOU OWE KUP A LOT, TOO, PROWL. OR HAS YOUR MEMORY OF BEING A LOWLY CADET SERVING UNDER HIM BEEN OVERWRITTEN BY YOUR EVER-UPGRADING PIPEWAD SUBROUTINE?
I'M NOT THE ONE IN DENIAL ABOUT MY PAST, SPRINGER.
THAT... THAT'S NOT THE ISSUE HERE...
CORRECT. THE ISSUE IS THIS CEASELESS FOLLY YOU LABEL A RESCUE MISSION.
WHY ARE YOU SO BENT ON RETRIEVING AN AUTOBOT WHOSE CEREBRAL PROCESSORS HAVE ROTTED AWAY FROM RADIATION POISONING, AND WHOSE BODY IS A SHAMBLING RELIC OF UNREPAIRABLE, INCOMPATIBLE JUNK?
HE'S ***LIVED*** HIS LIFE, SPRINGER. LET HIM GO.
NO! HE MEANS TOO MUCH!
TO YOU, MAYBE.
YOU SPARKLESS SPAWN OF A GLITCH. NOT JUST TO ME, TO EVERY AUTOBOT...
THE SAME AUTOBOTS WHO HAVE DIED NEEDLESSLY AT HIS HANDS? COME ON, SPRINGER. I'VE TURNED A BLIND EYE LONG ENOUGH.
IT'S ALL I CAN DO TO PREVENT OPTIMUS PRIME FROM LEARNING ABOUT THIS. HE'D ***NEVER*** APPROVE SUCH A MISSION.
IF YOU BELIEVED THAT FOR A NANO-SECOND, PROWL, YOU'D HAVE SQUEALED ALREADY.
BUT WE BOTH KNOW THAT IF YOU DID THAT, ***HE'D*** BE ON THAT PLANET RIGHT NOW WITHOUT A PLATE OF ANTI-RAD ARMOR ON HIM, DOING EVERYTHING TO BRING KUP HOME. RIGHT?
RIGHT?

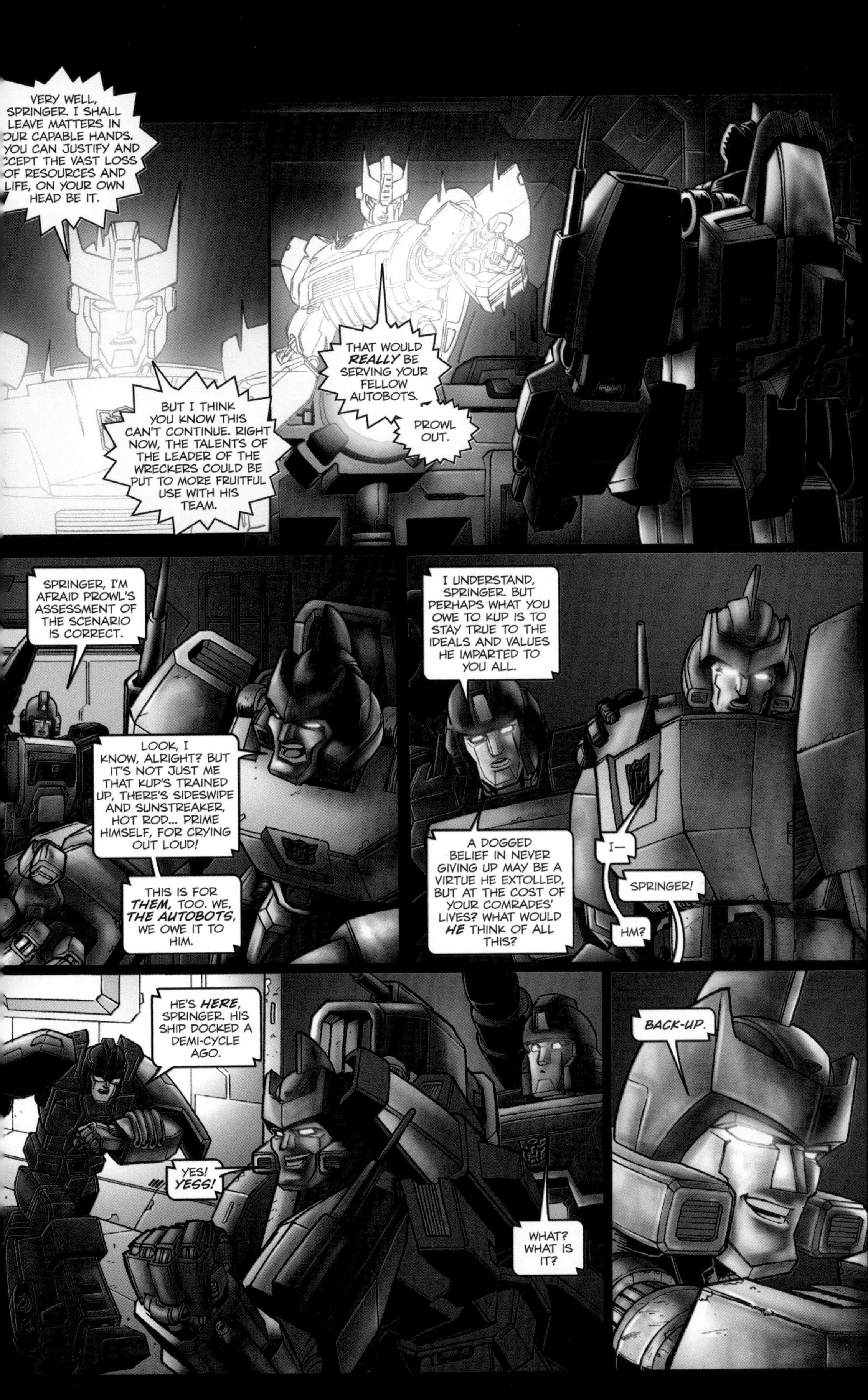
VERY WELL, SPRINGER. I SHALL LEAVE MATTERS IN OUR CAPABLE HANDS. YOU CAN JUSTIFY AND CCEPT THE VAST LOSS OF RESOURCES AND LIFE, ON YOUR OWN HEAD BE IT.
BUT I THINK YOU KNOW THIS CAN'T CONTINUE. RIGHT NOW, THE TALENTS OF THE LEADER OF THE WRECKERS COULD BE PUT TO MORE FRUITFUL USE WITH HIS TEAM.
THAT WOULD REALLY BE SERVING YOUR FELLOW AUTOBOTS.
PROWL OUT.
SPRINGER, I'M AFRAID PROWL'S ASSESSMENT OF THE SCENARIO IS CORRECT.
LOOK, I KNOW, ALRIGHT? BUT IT'S NOT JUST ME THAT KUP'S TRAINED UP, THERE'S SIDESWIPE AND SUNSTREAKER, HOT ROD... PRIME HIMSELF, FOR CRYING OUT LOUD!
THIS IS FOR THEM, TOO. WE, THE AUTOBOTS, WE OWE IT TO HIM.
I UNDERSTAND, SPRINGER. BUT PERHAPS WHAT YOU OWE TO KUP IS TO STAY TRUE TO THE IDEALS AND VALUES HE IMPARTED TO YOU ALL.
A DOGGED BELIEF IN NEVER GIVING UP MAY BE A VIRTUE HE EXTOLLED, BUT AT THE COST OF YOUR COMRADES' LIVES? WHAT WOULD HE THINK OF ALL THIS?
I—
SPRINGER!
HM?
HE'S HERE, SPRINGER. HIS SHIP DOCKED A DEMI-CYCLE AGO.
YES! YESS!
WHAT? WHAT IS IT?
BACK-UP.

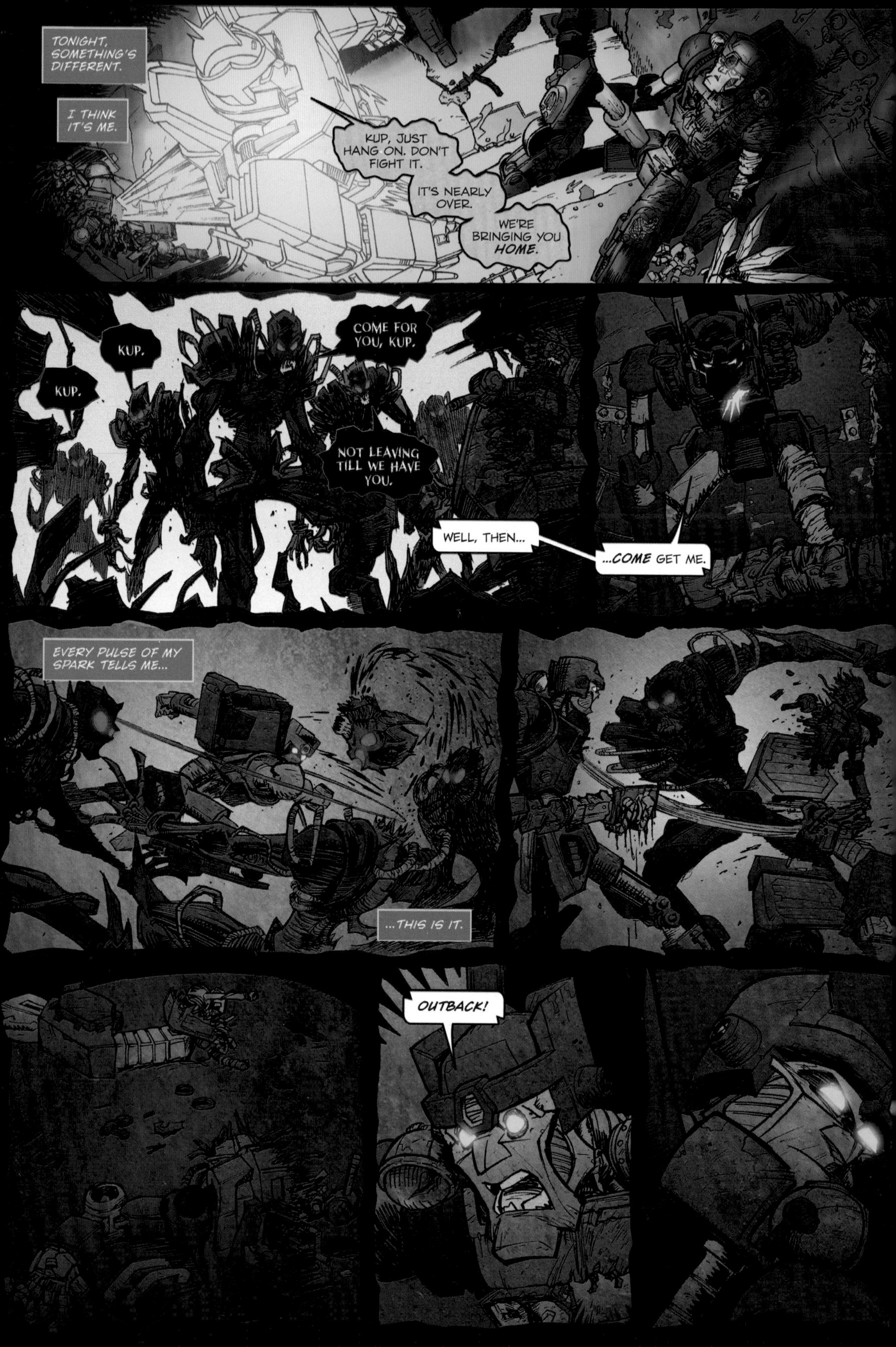
TONIGHT, SOMETHING'S DIFFERENT.
I THINK IT'S ME.
KUP, JUST HANG ON. DON'T FIGHT IT.
IT'S NEARLY OVER.
WE'RE BRINGING YOU HOME.
KUP.
KUP.
COME FOR YOU, KUP.
NOT LEAVING TILL WE HAVE YOU.
WELL, THEN...
...COME GET ME.
EVERY PULSE OF MY SPARK TELLS ME...
...THIS IS IT.
OUTBACK!

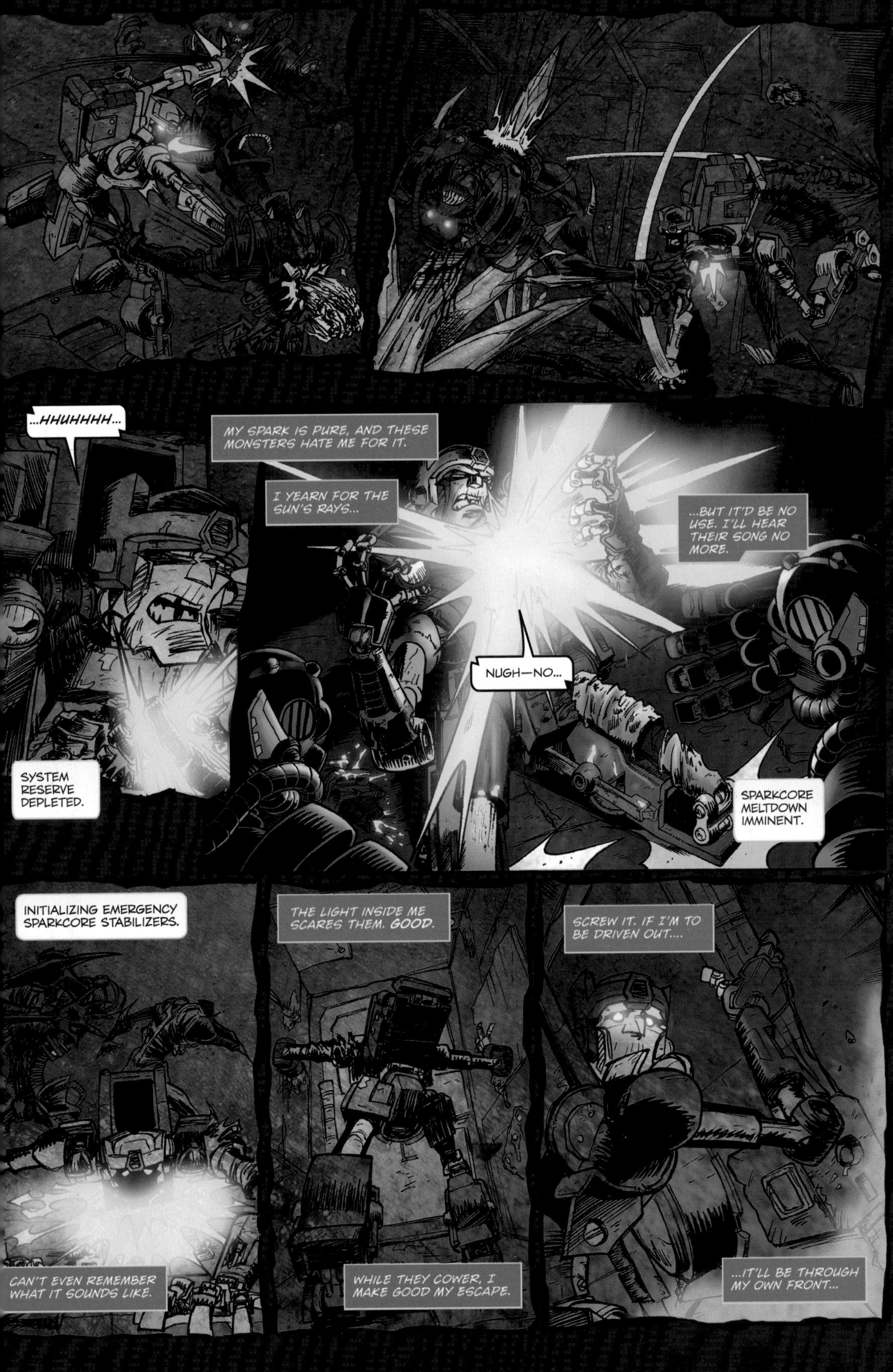
...HHUHHHH...
MY SPARK IS PURE, AND THESE MONSTERS HATE ME FOR IT.
I YEARN FOR THE SUN'S RAYS...
...BUT IT'D BE NO USE. I'LL HEAR THEIR SONG NO MORE.
NUGH—NO...
SYSTEM RESERVE DEPLETED.
SPARKCORE MELTDOWN IMMINENT.
INITIALIZING EMERGENCY SPARKCORE STABILIZERS.
CAN'T EVEN REMEMBER WHAT IT SOUNDS LIKE.
THE LIGHT INSIDE ME SCARES THEM. GOOD.
WHILE THEY COWER, I MAKE GOOD MY ESCAPE.
SCREW IT. IF I'M TO BE DRIVEN OUT....
...IT'LL BE THROUGH MY OWN FRONT...

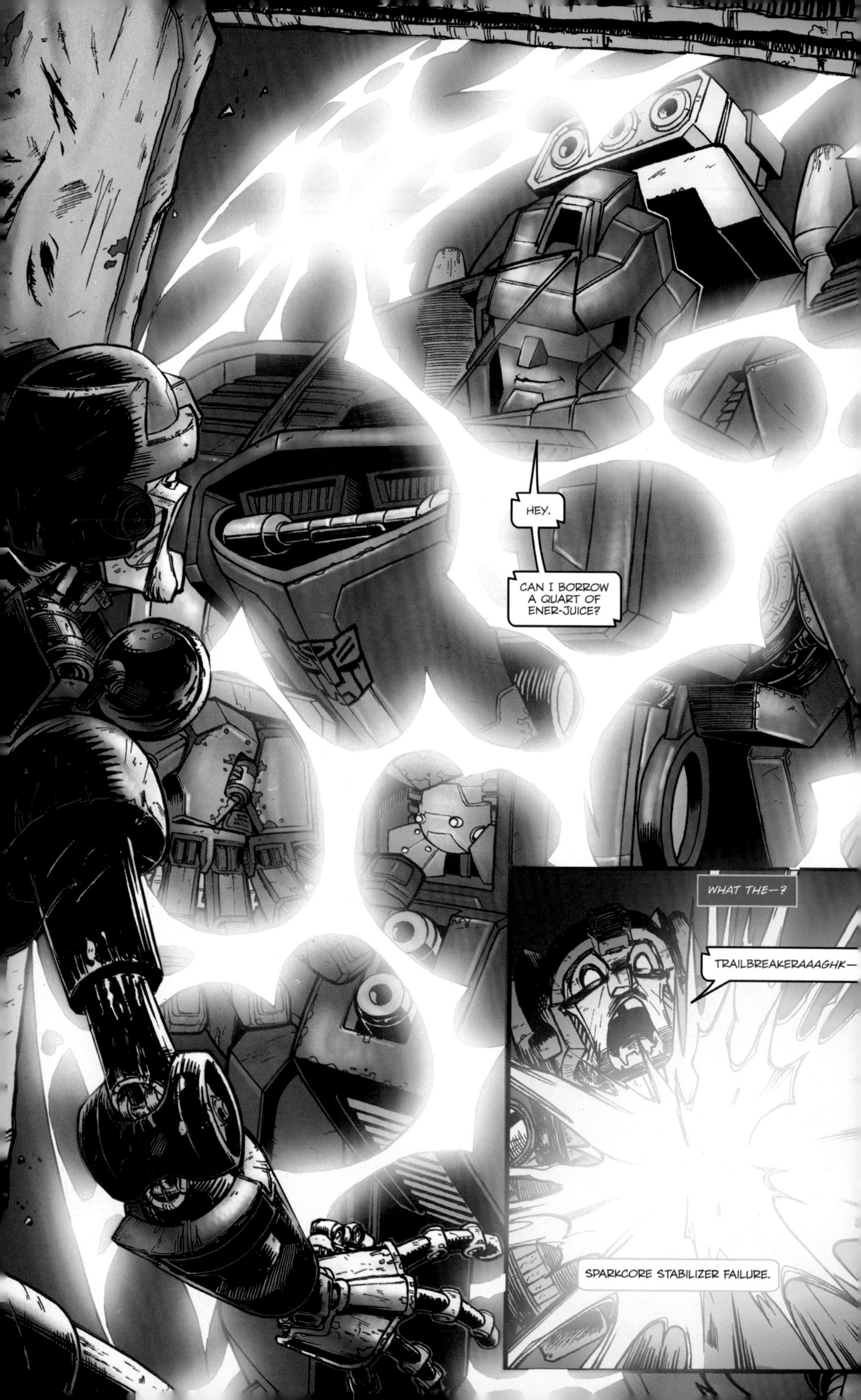
HEY.
CAN I BORROW A QUART OF ENER-JUICE?
WHAT THE—?
TRAILBREAKERAAAGHK—
SPARKCORE STABILIZER FAILURE.

MELTDOWN IMMINENT.
MELTDOWN IMMINENT.
MELTDOWN IMMINENT.

MELTDOWN IMMINENT.
MELTDOWN IMMI—

AW, *SLAG*. IT'S ALL GONNA GO *OFF*.

HANG ON...

NOT AFTER I WRAP *THIS* BAD BOY UP, IT AIN'T.

WH MP

HA! GOT IT! I GOT... KUP? *KUP*!

DAMN. *SPRINGER?* WE GOT AN EMERGENCY...

ORBITAL JUMP ACTIVATED.

KUP.

KUP...

WE GOT YOU, OLD-TIMER...

..WE GOT YOU.

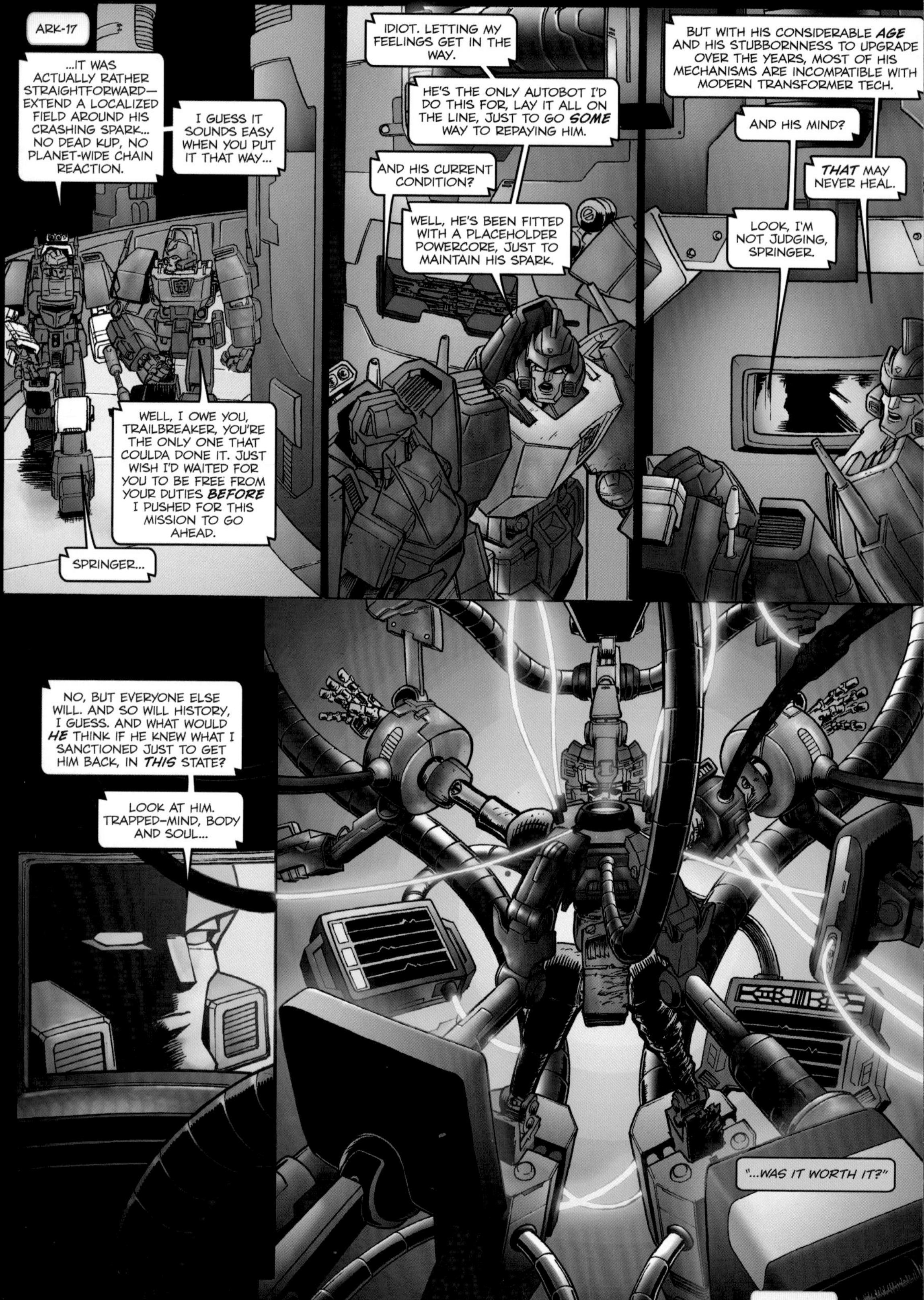
ARK-17
...IT WAS ACTUALLY RATHER STRAIGHTFORWARD—EXTEND A LOCALIZED FIELD AROUND HIS CRASHING SPARK... NO DEAD KUP, NO PLANET-WIDE CHAIN REACTION.
I GUESS IT SOUNDS EASY WHEN YOU PUT IT THAT WAY...
WELL, I OWE YOU, TRAILBREAKER, YOU'RE THE ONLY ONE THAT COULDA DONE IT. JUST WISH I'D WAITED FOR YOU TO BE FREE FROM YOUR DUTIES BEFORE I PUSHED FOR THIS MISSION TO GO AHEAD.
SPRINGER...
IDIOT. LETTING MY FEELINGS GET IN THE WAY.
HE'S THE ONLY AUTOBOT I'D DO THIS FOR, LAY IT ALL ON THE LINE, JUST TO GO SOME WAY TO REPAYING HIM.
AND HIS CURRENT CONDITION?
WELL, HE'S BEEN FITTED WITH A PLACEHOLDER POWERCORE, JUST TO MAINTAIN HIS SPARK.
BUT WITH HIS CONSIDERABLE AGE AND HIS STUBBORNNESS TO UPGRADE OVER THE YEARS, MOST OF HIS MECHANISMS ARE INCOMPATIBLE WITH MODERN TRANSFORMER TECH.
AND HIS MIND?
THAT MAY NEVER HEAL.
LOOK, I'M NOT JUDGING, SPRINGER.
NO, BUT EVERYONE ELSE WILL. AND SO WILL HISTORY, I GUESS. AND WHAT WOULD HE THINK IF HE KNEW WHAT I SANCTIONED JUST TO GET HIM BACK, IN THIS STATE?
LOOK AT HIM. TRAPPED—MIND, BODY AND SOUL...
"...WAS IT WORTH IT?"
THE END?